"WE WILL KEEP YOU SAFE."

SCREAM FOR US

ORDER OF THE UNSEEN

MOLLY DOYLE

Edited by The Havoc Archives
Blurb by The Havoc Archives
Cover design by DesignsbyCharlyy
Formatting by DesignsbyCharlyy

CONTENT WARNING

This is a Dark Romance/Suspense, Why Choose Novella. Scream For Us contains mature and graphic content that is not suitable for all audiences. Trigger warnings include: graphic sexually explicit scenes, physical assault, attempted sexual assault, mentions of self harm/bullying, blood/gore, mask kink, breath play/choking, knife play, fire play, raw sex/sex without a condom, praise/degradation kink, and murder.

DEDICATION

For those with a love for
Halloween...

But especially for those who
would love to be smashed like a
freaken pumpkin by three masked
men.

PLAYLIST

THE SUMMONING - SLEEP TOKEN
MIDDLE OF THE NIGHT - LOVELESS
A MATCH INTO WATER - PIERCE THE
VEIL
RUNRUNRUN - DUTCH MELROSE
JUST PRETEND - BAD OMENS
CHOKEHOLD - SLEEP TOKEN
MANIC - STRAY KIDS
SEX ON FIRE - KINGS OF LEON
TEAR YOU APART - SHE WANTS
REVENGE
FOR ME - LO NIGHTLY
DO I WANNA KNOW - ARCTIC
MONKEYS
REBEL YELL - BILLY IDOL

THE PRINCE IS NEVER GOING TO COME. EVERYONE KNOWS THAT; AND MAYBE SLEEPING BEAUTY'S DEAD.

- ANNE RICE

CHAPTER ONE

Jack-o'-lanterns are spread out along the sidewalk and leading up to the front door. I'm hypnotized by the flickering flames behind the precisely carved faces. Cobwebs cover the bushes, neon spotlights illuminate the front entrance, and there are bloody footprints spread across the pavement beneath my heels.

Music blasts through the house as I enter, along with a thick layer of smoke from a fog machine hidden beside the door, creeping its way across the floor. There are people in costumes everywhere. They weren't kidding when they said this Halloween party would go down in Salem history.

It was a bad idea to come here alone. A cold shiver shoots down my spine at the thought. I swiftly turn on my heel to make my exit, but Jenna nearly knocks me backward.

"Quinn!" she exclaims, vodka on her breath, as she grabs onto my arms to keep herself steady. "You're here!"

"Somehow."

"I had no idea you were coming," she drunkenly babbles. "I'm so glad you're here."

She's probably shocked to see me at a party, instead of my typical penchant for avoiding social gatherings.

"Have you seen Stacy?" she asks.

"Not yet. I just got here," I tell her. "Sorry."

With that, she scurries away.

Making my way down the crowded hallway and into the kitchen, loud conversations drown out the music from the other rooms. Flickering candles create the perfect amount of light for me to figure out my options for booze.

Beer. *More* beer. Hard liquor.

Spooky party punch, it is.

"Good choice," a voice says as its owner enters my view. "Really does pack a *punch*."

Snorting, I roll my eyes. "The stronger the better," I say, nearly overflowing my solo cup in the process. "Cool Joker makeup."

"Thanks." He raises an eyebrow. "What are you supposed to be?"

Glancing down at my outfit, I cringe. This was my last-minute effort to try to throw a costume together, except I still have no idea who or what I am. All I could come up with is a tight black corset bodysuit, fishnet tights, and black combat heels.

"That's a great question," I sheepishly reply.

"Kevin," someone calls from across the room. "You coming with us?"

Joker looks their way and nods, before turning back to me. "What's your name again?"

"Quinn."

"See you around, Quinn."

The Halloween punch did in fact, *pack a punch.* Joker was right.

A thin film of fog creeps its way from the ground, surrounding everyone on the dance floor. Making my way to the center of the room, I sway my hips to the beat of the music, enticed by the strobe lights that seem to be coming from every direction. Lifting my arms into the air and shutting my eyes, I submit to the new carefree feeling that works its way through me.

Thank God for alcohol in social settings.

Suddenly, hands are on my waist, guiding me to the rhythm. I continue to dance, not giving any thought to the person behind me, until they slip their hands to the front of me.

Lower.

Lower.

Swatting them away, an uncomfortable feeling creeps up on me, although I pay it no mind at first. Until they grab onto me, forcing themselves against my body. Groping my breasts, trailing their hand down to my lower waist.

"Stop," I rush out, trying to pull away.

They breathe heavily against my ear. "You like it?"

"No, you creep," I shoot back.

They're too strong.

"No! No! Stop!"

Sloppily kissing my neck, they attempt slipping their fingers beneath the material of my corset. Finally, I break free from their grasp, bumping into several people dancing beside us. To my dismay, they ignore us entirely. My heart hammers. There are so many people. It's too loud. The smoke is so thick, I can hardly see, let alone breathe.

Turning to face the person who wouldn't accept no for an answer, anger and disgust consume me. He steps forward, reaching out for me again. Slamming my hands against his chest, I shove him away, and this time he gets the hint.

It's clear that he has taken offense to my rejection. His eyes turn dark. Cold. He becomes as still as stone. Fear settles in, and before I can even make sense of it, he's grabbing a red plastic cup from someone's hand.

Within seconds, my chest is drenched with beer. My jaw nearly drops as I stare at him in disbelief, horrified that he just splashed a drink in my face.

"Bitch," he laughs.

A tall dark figure lurks from the corner of my eye. Suddenly, he has my assaulter on the ground, and he's towering over him. Leaning down, he slams his gloved fists against the man's face.

Over and over.

He grabs him by the throat. "If you ever fucking touch her

again, I'll put you down like a sick dog."

You can almost hear the sound of his face crunching from each blow while blood pours from his nose like a faucet.

Lyrics boom from the speakers.

I can't wait to hear you—

I can't wait to hear you scream.

Everyone scurries out of the way, watching in fear as the scene unfolds right before our eyes. Several people try to step in to help de-escalate the situation. But as soon as they try to pull him off, he jerks toward them, taunting them.

They immediately step back, not daring to be his next target.

My heart is pounding against my ribcage, and I finally realize that this was all for me. He helped me. He *protected* me.

His silhouette is daunting. Primitive. It's as if he's hunting his prey, and he doesn't stop beating him until he's knocked out cold.

The figure dressed in all black slowly turns to face me, and the moment I see the mask from *Scream* hiding his identity, I'm left a hot, quivering mess.

There's just something about this moment that mesmerizes me. He approaches me, now towering over my small frame. He's at least six foot three, and even though the dark fabric of his costume hides his body, it's obvious he's built like a god.

He tilts his head to the side, studying my reaction, and my body reacts right on cue. My nipples pucker, straining against the material of my corset. My inner thighs become drenched. My face is flushed, and my breathing is labored.

"Thank you," I blurt out.

"His face!" a guy in cowboy attire shouts, kneeling over my assaulter, who is still bleeding and unconscious. "You broke his face, man! I'll kill you!"

Ghost snaps his head in his direction.

The cowboy rushes to his feet, bolting toward us, when fear overtakes me. With one swift motion, Ghost swings, and his fist collides with the cowboy's jaw.

He collapses onto the floor and remains there, motionless.

Everyone begins to scream. It's a real life bloodbath, and I'm frozen.

Another figure appears from the corner of my eye, bringing me back to reality. They grab onto Ghost's shoulders, trying their best to hold him back. It then becomes evident that the two of them know each other.

Without thinking it through, I push my way through the crowd of people—some laughing, some crying—and I lock my fingers around Ghost's wrist. He looks back to his friend, who is wearing a *Jason Voorhees* mask, and they both nod.

Pulling him along with me as we exit the room, we turn a corner, nearly knocking someone onto their ass. Once we spot a large spiral staircase, I lead him to the top. It's much darker on this floor, but less crowded, and the music only seems to grow louder. It echoes through the hallway, sounding like a beating heart.

Thump-thump. Thump-thump.

Thump-thump. Thump-thump.

Pushing open the nearest door, I stumble over a pair of shoes. Before I fall, Ghost catches me, bringing me close to his chest. He's so firm. Masculine. Staring up at him through my lashes, I gaze helplessly into the large eyes of his mask.

Jason closes the door behind us.

Here I am, alone with Ghost and Jason—two people I've never met. Yet, I've never felt so safe.

What does that say about me?

There's red-hot sexual tension, an electrical current in the air, and my inner thighs once again become slick.

Well, *shit*.

I'm infatuated.

Maybe it's because Ghost is nearly crushing me against his body, and his cologne smells so goddamn seductive it makes my head spin. Or maybe it's the fact that he just beat the shit out of some guy who wouldn't take his hands off me when I told him to stop.

Suddenly the rush of adrenaline makes me feel sick, and I peel myself away from him.

"There was so much blood," I stutter, attempting to run my hand through my hair. It's a sticky, tangled mess from the beer that was splashed in my face.

"You good?" Ghost asks me.

That *voice*. So powerful, so throaty. It makes me weak.

"Yeah," I say, brushing out a knot with my fingers. "I'm fine."

"I have this urge to kill—" he hesitates, his voice low. "—anyone who touches you."

My eyes widen and my lips part in a silent gasp.

Holy shit. Did he really just say that?

"Do I know you?" I ask.

He steps forward, closing the small space between us. "Where's the fun in that?"

"I don't recognize your voice," I let out.

With that, he turns toward his friend.

The mask he's wearing is frightening. I've never been a huge fan of *Friday the 13th*, or any horror films in general. Yet there's something about his broody, mysterious presence that has me completely aroused.

He's tall, although a bit shorter than Ghost, but his build is huge. Even though he's wearing a bulky jacket, it's not hard to tell.

"Did that guy hurt you?" Jason asks.

His voice sends a chill down my spine. God help me.

Although there's a voice in my head that says, *"God isn't here right now."*

Now I know how Elena Gilbert felt, torn between two men.

"No. He didn't have the chance to hurt me," I anxiously reply, gazing up at Ghost with gratitude. "Thanks to you."

"He knows what he wants," Jason speaks up.

"Oh?" I question, taken aback. "And what does he want, exactly?"

Ghost steps toward me, inching closer. Staring up at his mask, I swallow hard.

"Don't ask him, little Quinn," Ghost says. "Ask me directly."

A warm, fuzzy feeling washes over me from his seductive tone. "What do you want?" I finally ask, barely any sound to my voice.

"Silly girl. I want what every other guy in this party wants."

He reaches out to touch my hair, brushing it over my

shoulder, his leather gloves lightly rubbing against my neck. I feel so exposed as he stands over me.

Vulnerable.

"Say it," I urge, gathering the robe over his chest in my hands. "Tell me what you want."

"Fuck," he breathes. "Feisty little thing, aren't you?"

Without warning, the door opens, slamming against the wall with a loud thud. The music pours into the room, completely ruining the moment.

Someone dressed as *Michael Myers* stands in the doorway. How are they all taller than six feet? I've been reading too many smut books lately, and I clearly haven't gotten out enough.

"Got your text," Michael says, revealing that he's with them.

"Couldn't have been any better with your timing," Ghost dryly mutters, dismissing them with a single wave of his hand.

The second the door shuts behind them, he gazes down at me in silence. I can almost make out the outline of his eyes from the dim light on the other side of the room. Suddenly, my heart begins to pound at the thought of us finally being alone with one another.

What am I doing? What am I *thinking*?

This is so unlike me.

But that's the thing. Tonight I can be whoever the hell I want to be.

And for once in my life, I choose to be reckless.

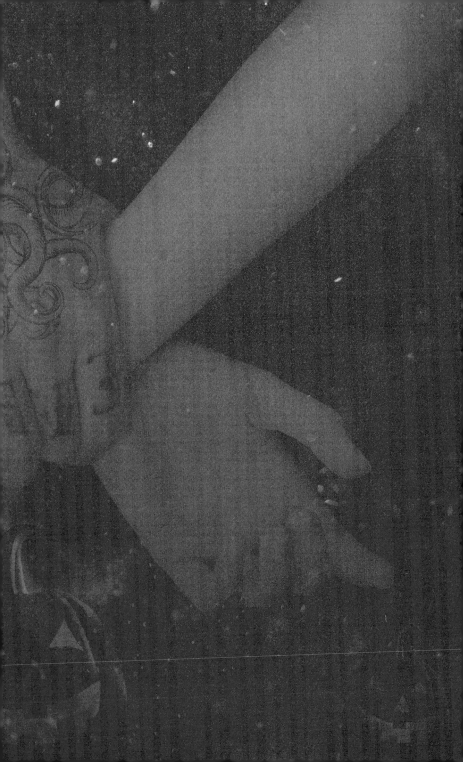

CHAPTER TWO

You asked what I want," Ghost says, inching closer as I lose my ability to breathe. "I've been watching you all goddamn night. I want to fuck the sadness out of you until you're screaming in ecstasy while coming around my cock."

A hushed moan escapes my trembling lips as he lights a burning desire within me. I've never felt this way before. So hot and undeniably bothered. An ache settles between my legs, and warmth blushes over my skin. I can literally feel my clit pulsing, begging for his tongue, and I am barely fighting off the urge to tear off his costume.

"I want to explore every inch of that sexy little body you

got there," he continues. "Such a sexy piece of ass you are, *little Quinn*."

Another quiet moan leaves my lips without my permission.

"You like it when I call you that, don't you, baby?"

"Little Quinn," I echo his words.

"There it is," he coos, taking my jaw in his hand, ensuring I look directly into the eyes of his mask. "Now tell me. If I were to slip my hand between your thighs right now, how wet would you be for me?"

My abdomen clenches at the thought.

The truth is, I'm more wet now than I've ever been in my life.

"Very," I whisper.

"Fuck," he grunts, tightening his grip on my face, squishing my cheeks. "Even through this mask I can already smell how sweet you are. I want a taste."

My knees are only moments from buckling. My entire body begins to quiver. My face fills with heat.

Somehow my darkest fantasies—ones that I figured I could only dream or read about—have the power to come to life right before my eyes.

"Such a pretty mouth. Put it to good use." He traces my bottom lip with his thumb, cocking his head to the side. "Tell me what you want from me, and I'll give it to you."

And finally, I let go wholeheartedly.

"You," I answer.

"Do you?"

"Yes. I want you to bring my darkest fantasies to life."

"Darkest," he echoes, hesitating. "I can imagine my *dark* is far different than yours, sweetheart."

"Dark," I emphasize. "But there's one condition."

Placing his hand on my chest, he moves me backward, pinning me to the wall. Lightly wrapping his fingers around my throat, he presses down, making it a challenge for me to swallow.

"Tonight," I rush out, grasping his wrist. "Just one night."

"One night?"

"Yes. By sunrise, it's over."

He laughs, with no humor intended. "You say that so easily, like it's possible for me to let you go."

"Well, that's my condition," I press.

"Even if it's for tonight, and tonight *only*, little Quinn," he hesitates, spreading my legs with his knee. "You'll still always be mine."

Blinking up at him, I say nothing.

"Mercy," he lets out. "Beg me for mercy if my *dark* is too much for you to bear."

Ghost releases me, and I gasp for air, watching as he removes the belt of his robe. I try to imagine what hides beneath the long, draped sleeves and shredded fabric of his costume.

"Face the wall," he instructs.

And I hesitate, unsure if I've heard him correctly.

"Don't make me repeat myself, Quinn," he warns, his voice low. Tight. "You asked for dark. Don't forget that."

Turning on my heel, I stare at the wall, bracing myself for the unknown. I'm terrified, yet thrilled at the same time. Adrenaline pumps like nitrous through my veins.

I want this.

I *need* this.

He lets out a sharp breath. "Hands against the wall."

Pressing my palms against the cold, hard surface, a chill creeps down my spine.

My instinct is telling me to run far away.

Except my arousal is evident. My nipples are puckered into hard, red buds. My pale skin is flushed. My breathing is shallow. My body is begging to be railed. Destroyed. In every way.

But not just by anyone.

By *him.*

Ghost.

"Do you trust me?" he asks, and I can almost feel his gaze burning through the back of my skull.

"Yes," I answer softly.

"Foolish, little Quinn," he taunts me, brushing my hair behind my shoulder, exposing my neck. "Wrong answer."

I frown, questioning my morals.

It's Halloween. It's time to be reckless. Be reckless.

I spin around until I'm facing him, defying his orders entirely. He towers over me, even with the added inches of my heels, making me feel so powerless in his presence. So weak and defenseless.

It's disturbing, yet so hot it has my mouth salivating. I'm *dying* to know what it feels like to be his.

"I want you," I admit, pleading with my eyes for him to act. "Right now."

Ghost leans into me, pressing my back to the wall. "So eager," he says, as I wait impatiently for him to finally remove his mask. He drapes the belt of his costume over his shoulders and slips off his gloves.

And *those hands.*

They're huge—thick and veiny. It's uncanny how wide his palm is and how long his fingers are. He's not a boy. He's a man, in every sense of the word.

A god.

A devil, maybe.

My imagination wanders…

He tosses his gloves to the floor and retrieves the belt, holding it out before me at eye level. "Close your eyes," he orders.

I obey, feeling the soft fabric as it rests over my eyelids, cutting out the dim light.

He slips his hand between my thighs, massaging my clit over the thin fabric of my bodysuit, making me squirm. "Such a good girl."

CHAPTER THREE

The quiet *rip* of my fishnets being torn at my crotch leaves me on edge. I can't even fathom how hot he must look on his knees for me. My legs begin to quiver, and I mentally applaud myself for deciding to not wear any panties tonight.

The cold air sends a chill through me as Ghost spreads my legs wider, exposing me.

"Please," I whimper, taking my bottom lip between my teeth.

"That's right," he bites out. "Fucking beg."

My heart pounds through my ribcage. "Please…" I'm desperate to release all this built-up sexual tension.

His warm breath brushes my clit, every nerve ending on edge. "Yes," he groans, pushing his fingers between my sensitive flesh. "Such a needy little slut, aren't you?"

My body jolts, and I helplessly writhe against the wall, reaching down for him. Burying my fingers through his thick, lush hair, I kick open my legs wider.

"Please, please, please," I beg.

"Please, I'm begging you." He whines back, mocking me. "Fuck." He rubs my clit in slow, torturous circles, as I moan with satisfaction. "You're so fucking wet."

He dips the tip of his finger inside me, and the anticipation is beyond agonizing. Thrusting deeper, my inner walls tighten around him, and my stomach tenses. Without warning, he quickens his pace, pushing his finger into me over and over, before adding in another.

Curling his fingers in all the right places, he slows, stroking my walls. "Such a tight, little cunt," he says.

"*Ghost*," I impatiently moan.

That does it.

He lifts me into his arms and lowers me onto the bed. Firmly grabbing my ankles, he pulls me to the edge, spreading my legs once more. He teasingly presses his lips on the sensitive skin of my inner thigh.

Finally, he takes me into his mouth. He traces his tongue over my clit, flicking lightly in the perfect rhythm.

Oh hell, he knows what he's doing.

Nobody has *ever* made me feel this good.

He skims his hands over my breasts, and I grab his wrists, holding them in place. Yanking down my top ever so slightly, he pinches my nipples, twirling them between his fingers. This only seems to bring me more pleasure, as he thrusts his tongue inside of my core.

"Oh my God," I moan, writhing against his face. "*Yes*."

He trails his hands down my chest, ribcage, and hips, caressing each part of my body as he slips them lower and lower to my most sensitive place. Moving my legs further apart with one hand, he pushes two fingers inside of me with the other.

Thrust after thrust, he continues this beautiful attack of sucking, nibbling, and tasting. He's savoring me, as if he's literally starving.

My stomach flutters, my breathing quickens, and I buck my hips, matching the thrusts of his fingers. Wrapping his muscular arms beneath my legs, he reaches for my arms, suddenly pinning me to the bed, giving me no option to escape.

Fisting the sheets with my trembling, sweaty hands, a feeling builds up inside me, and then bursts into pieces. I come undone—forgetting to breathe, toes curling. Riding out my orgasm, I grind myself against his face, until I physically can't take it anymore.

"Fuck," he groans, his face still buried against my wetness. "You taste too good, baby. I need more."

He tightens his hold on my arms, pinning me in place, and burying his face against my pussy. Just when I believe that it isn't possible to come again, he proves me wrong, fucking me into oblivion with his fingers and tongue until I'm exploding with pleasure, seeing stars through my eyelids.

"I can't," I whimper, trying to break free from his grasp.

Within seconds, loud music from the party bursts through the room, and my heart nearly leaps into my throat. The door must have opened. Except Ghost doesn't stop.

There's a loud thud of the door closing, and the beautiful torment continues.

"I can't take anymore," I gasp. Hushed, little whimpers escape my lips. "Oh, yes. *Yes*."

My climax consumes me, taking over entirely. Nothing else matters but the earth-shattering sensations, as I ride out wave after wave of this everlasting euphoria. My inner walls spasm, my legs begin to shake, and I'm sure I've forgotten to breathe.

Ghost finally releases me, and I remain motionless on the bed, attempting to gather back any strength in my body that I can find. A short time passes before I feel his leather gloves caressing my face.

"Mine," he claims. "You are *mine*."

He unties the belt of his costume that has acted as a blindfold from around my head. Slowly opening my eyes, they adjust to the light, and my heart drops the moment I notice Jason and Michael in the corner of the room.

"Wait," I rush out, quickly trying to cover myself. "They were watching?"

Ghost turns to face me, pulling on his menacing *Scream* mask before I have the chance to see his face.

He nods.

I blink up at him in silence, shocked.

He gazes down at me. "You're upset," he observes. "What part of *dark fantasies* doesn't involve having other guys watch as you get that sweet little cunt of yours eaten?"

My lips part and my stomach flutters. I can't find the right words.

Ghost steps closer to the bed, and reaches down, lightly stroking my hair. "Just because you're *mine*, little Quinn, doesn't mean I won't share," he says. "But only if that's what *you* want."

Many thoughts cross my mind, and I get that feeling that I can't seem to get enough of. Is this what I want?

Yes, I scream at myself.

When suddenly, the door slams open. Several guys dressed as football players stumble into the room, and they fortunately fail to notice as I quickly button up the bottom of my bodysuit.

The moment they acknowledge our presence and that the room is occupied, a sly look appears on their faces. It's immediately clear they have the wrong idea.

Jason makes his way to the side of the bed where Ghost stands on edge.

"Hell yeah," one of them exclaims.

"What's going on in here, boys?" another one asks, his tone threatening.

"A damn good time," another one drunkenly slurs, closing the door behind him. "We taking turns on her?"

Jason immediately grasps my arm, pulling me to my feet, and practically tosses me behind the three of them to shield me.

"What the fuck did you just say?" Ghost asks.

Something is wrong. Very wrong. From the tone of his voice, it almost comes out as a challenge. His entire demeanor changes in an instant, as his hands ball into fists at his sides.

He's ready.

Ready to hurt them.

Or *worse.*

"No," I loudly gasp, pushing past Jason and standing in front of Ghost, blocking his way. "I want to dance."

He looks down, fixating his attention on me. Yet he remains silent. Unsure.

"Let's go," I say, taking his large, gloved hand and linking my fingers through his.

The football players stare at us as we walk by, completely dumbfounded, and I pray that they keep their mouths shut for their sake as I open the door.

We make our way through the doorway, until one of them laughs. "Whatever. We'll find her later and have our own fun."

Ghost and Michael turn around, barging back into the room, as Jason stands on guard with me in the almost empty hallway. Fists are flying, shouts echo over the loud music, and my heart drops the second I see Ghost holding one of them against the wall.

The sharp silver knife is pressed against the guy's throat, and everyone becomes paralyzed with fear. He leans closer, and although I can't make out what he says, I know it's bad.

The guy's face turns green, like he's on the verge of being sick.

He holds up his hands, trembling. "I'm sorry. I'm sorry," he repeats, cowering before him.

Ghost lowers his hand, putting away the knife, and finally I can breathe again. Despite the thrill of being protected from vile and drunk frat guys, there is a part of me that believes even if I wasn't standing here, this still wouldn't have gone any differently.

The hit comes much quicker than I could have expected. With tremendous force, Ghost's fist collides with his nose, an eerie *crunch* sounding on impact.

The football player stumbles backward, drops to the floor, and cradles his face with his hands.

The moment his friends make a move to have his back, he shouts at them. "Leave it alone!" He doesn't move an inch. "Just leave it alone."

Ghost and Michael stare down at him, still as stone, and time feels as if it has stopped. A sinister feeling washes over me. These frat guys would have sexually assaulted me if they had been given the chance.

If it wasn't for Ghost, Jason, and Michael.

My breathing hitches as pure hatred boils in my veins, until Jason's hand on my shoulder brings me back to reality. I gaze up at him, staring passionately into the eyes of his mask, and he *knows*. It's as if he's read my mind.

Bringing me against his chest, I nuzzle my face into his bulky jacket, and my eyes flutter shut. He holds the back of my head, gently stroking my hair, calming me.

"You're safe," he promises, and even with his deep, menacing tone, he eases my fears. "And *ours*."

CHAPTER FOUR

Although some people choose to dress up as monsters on Halloween night, others simply *are* monsters. Even over the loud music erupting from the surround sound speakers, the wind howls as it gusts through the open front doors of the house.

More people crowd into the entryway, dressed in a mixture of scary and sexy costumes, smeared in face paint and fake blood. There's a creepy glow created from the neon lights draped from the ceiling, surrounded by bat and pumpkin décor.

My mind becomes overstimulated as I scan everyone in my path. I'm suddenly dying for a stiff drink, ready for the night to *truly* begin. The truth is, I've never felt more alive.

Candles flicker in the dim kitchen light, spread out across the countertops, showcasing the delicious party treats. There are Halloween-inspired cupcakes, *Jack Skellington* chocolate sandwich cookie pops, and white chocolate-covered strawberries decorated as ghosts.

There's a large, spiderweb covered, ice-filled bowl that holds fake blood bags containing dark red alcohol. The bucket beside it holds large syringes, filled with many colors of different gelatin dessert flavors. They couldn't have been more festive.

"Blue raspberry," a girl's voice shrieks, as she swoops in front of me and grabs the last blue syringe. "Quinn," she murmurs, catching me off guard.

It's Veronica.

The girl who completely ruined my middle and high school experiences.

My body stiffens, and I can't find it in me to breathe. Awful memories flood through my mind—being bullied, the rumors that were spread around about me, and the harassment I had to face every single day. Being subjected to bullying on every social media platform known to man is the reason I couldn't have a cell phone or computer growing up.

More flashbacks race toward me.

Crying myself to sleep, night after night.

My wrists. Razorblades. *Blood*.

Veronica and her friends—both guys and girls—constantly telling me that my father had killed himself because I was born. Telling everyone he was so repulsed having me as a daughter that he took his own life.

"I haven't seen you in a few years," she awkwardly says, forcing a phony smile.

"Yeah," I agree, trembling.

Ghost wraps his arm around my shoulder, bringing me against his firm chest, and I relax in his embrace.

"Oh, you're with someone," Veronica points out, sounding appalled, which triggers me.

"She's with *us*," Jason clarifies, tucking a strand of my hair behind my ear.

Michael steps beside us, remaining silent, but making himself known.

Her face drops at the realization.

Suddenly, I've never felt more confident. After these last few years, starting over and learning to be happy with the life I was given, I remember the promise I made to myself.

To never allow any of my bullies to ever affect me again.

"You took the last one," I observe, eyeing her gelatin shot. "Bummer. Blue raspberry is my favorite."

"That sucks," she remarks, her jaw tightening.

"Give it to her," Michael orders, and I am blown away.

She scowls. "What?"

"He said, *give it to me*," I repeat his words, stepping forward until I'm mere inches away. "But you know what," I say, hesitating briefly, before taking a cherry-flavored one from the bucket. "I think I'm good. I'm really good, actually. Never been better."

Pressing my lips around the tip of the syringe, I shoot the gelatin into my mouth, savoring the taste of vodka that burns the back of my throat.

"I wish I could say it was good to see you, Veronica," I

say, tossing the empty syringe into the nearest trash bin. "But it wasn't."

Her mouth falls wide open.

Swiftly turning on my heel, I head toward the nearest bathroom.

"I've changed, Quinn!" she calls after me, almost trying to convince herself.

"I hope you have," I shout back emotionally, meaning it from the bottom of my heart.

Pushing open the bathroom door and stumbling inside, I firmly grip the edge of the sink to keep myself upright. My chest tightens, my heart accelerates, and out of nowhere I feel faint. Not another panic attack. Not tonight.

The small room begins to spin in circles around me, and I feel a sense of detachment from the world around me.

Fuck you, crippling anxiety.

"Are you okay?" Ghost asks, catching me off guard.

"The door," I rush out, breathlessly. "Please shut the door."

Taking in a deep breath and closing my eyes, embarrassment washes over me. I can't believe he's seeing me like this, at my lowest amid an anxiety attack.

"What did she do to you?" There's barely any sound to his voice.

"Nothing," I whisper, tightly gripping the edge of the sink.

"Quinn—"

"Nothing," I sternly repeat. "It was nothing."

"Alright," he says, the door creaking open. "I'll give you space."

"No," I gasp, looking into the mirror and locking my gaze on him, completely unbothered by the creepy mask in the reflection. "I don't want space."

He shuts the door, his hand lingering on the doorknob. After a moment, he cautiously approaches me.

"What *do* you want?" he asks, testing me, pressing the solid frame of the front of his body against my backside. "Do you want to talk?"

Shaking my head, I softly respond, "No."

"Then, what? Use your words, little Quinn."

"A distraction. I want a distraction."

Reaching around to the front of my chest, he locks his gloved hand around my throat, holding me still. "Like this?" he breathes, tightening his grasp.

I nod slightly.

Leaning down, he hesitates beside my ear. "Your words, Quinn."

"Yes," I mutter. "More."

Trailing his hand to my jaw, he turns my head to the side, forcing me to look at him. In the right lighting, I'm almost able to get a glimpse of his eyes through the black mesh covering the dark holes of his mask.

Almost.

He turns me around and leans down, gripping beneath my thighs before lifting me from the floor. He eases me onto the cold, hard surface of the sink.

"This?" he asks.

"More," I whisper.

"I know what you want, but I love to hear you *beg*."

Lightly brushing his hands against the back of my legs, then trailing the tips of his fingers to my inner thighs, he hesitates at the lower buttons of my bodysuit.

"Please," I moan, feeling his broad, manly shoulders beneath my hands. "Please, more."

"You call that *begging*?"

"Please," I plead, as he rubs my clit over the thin fabric. "Please, Ghost, please."

"Fuck, baby," he sharply exhales. "That's right. Say my name."

"*Ghost.*"

"Are you on birth control?"

"Yes," I reply, shaking my head once I see the foil packet he's retrieved from his pocket. "I was recently tested and I'm clean. Are you?"

He nods, tossing it onto the counter.

"Now distract me," I order.

He groans. Tearing open the buttons at my crotch and lifting the robe of his costume, he yanks down his pants, keeping them right below his ass. His thick, hard cock is already slick with desire, and so impressively big.

Holy shit. There's no way I can take him.

As I brace on his shoulders, he pulls me to the very edge of the sink, rubbing the tip of his cock along my wet entrance. Up and down, over and over, toying with me. Teasing me. Driving me to the brink of insanity.

"Please," I eagerly beg, desperate to feel him.

Without warning, Ghost enters me with one, hard thrust. Stretching me wide as he buries himself to the hilt.

"Fuck," he bites out, getting a better grip on me as he secures his arms around my back.

The inner walls of my core tighten and grip at his cock with each stroke, and my body jolts back from the hard force. Thrust, after thrust, after thrust, he fucks me without emotion. Plunging himself deeper, faster, he pushes his way inside of me repeatedly.

Wrapping my arms around his neck, I hold onto him for dear life, spreading my legs wider so I can feel him more fully. It's almost too much.

He's too massive.

There's the sound of skin smacking intermingled with moans of praise as he quickens his pace, pounding into me relentlessly. Crying out to him, whimpering, and gasping for air to fill my deprived lungs, I slip my hands under his robe, tracing the muscles of his back. I dig my nails all the way down the flesh of his back before taking his firm ass in my hands.

"Yes," I cry out, throwing back my head, matching his merciless thrusts with my hips. "Oh, fuck, yes. Yes. Yes!"

My eyes start to close as my climax builds, rapidly approaching.

"Look at me," he savagely orders, slamming into me.

Hard.

Harder.

Even harder.

I obey, staring desperately into the dark eyes of his mask. Something about this is so erotic, so twisted. Here I am, in a stranger's bathroom, getting railed by *Ghostface.*

And even better, he's fucking my brains out through the hole he ripped in my fishnets.

Please don't kill me Mr. Ghostface. Not yet, at least.

Roughly squeezing my ass, and bruising my skin, he lifts me from the sink. Standing strong and tall, he bounces me on his thick, hard shaft. Adjusting to his size in this new position, my arms find their way around his neck. I cry out in ecstasy, grinding my clit against his pelvis, creating the perfect amount of friction.

"Yes," I whimper, rubbing myself against him.

He brings me down harder each time, bucking his hips with each deliberate thrust, throwing me closer and closer to the edge.

"Fuck," he groans, slamming my back against the wall.

Wincing from the pain, my legs lock tighter around his waist. I cry out, moaning louder, and he claims me ruthlessly.

"Yes, baby. I want to hear you scream."

No longer able to hold myself back, I scream out with pleasure, letting go completely.

"Good girl," he praises, squeezing my ass as he slams into me with urgency. "You're such a good fucking girl."

"Yes," I whimper, as he nuzzles his mask into the crook of my neck, adjusts his angle, and sinks into me deeper. "God, yes!"

"I want everyone in this house to know that you're mine."

"Yes!"

"Tell them, baby."

"I'm yours," I breathlessly moan, rocking my hips to match his thrusts. "Yes!"

"That's right. Such a good little slut. Bounce on daddy's dick."

Tightly gripping his shoulders, I ride his pulsating cock, breathing in the heady scent of his cologne. The seductive aroma washes over me, and my senses are heightened, sending me into a state of pure euphoria. He pulls me from the wall, easing me up and down on his thickness.

"Fuck," he grunts, bringing me down harder. "Just like that."

"Ghost," I moan, right on the edge.

"Come for me," he urges.

My orgasm rips through me, catching me completely off guard. The intensity is unimaginable. I've only ever gotten off with my vibrator, but Ghost hits all the right places.

My back arches, pleasure consuming my body from my head to my toes. In this moment, nothing else matters. As he slowly moves within me, he grips me tighter, gaining back full control.

Pure bliss takes over—earth-shattering sensations rocking through me like nothing I've ever felt in my life.

This is what it's supposed to feel like.

"Fuck," he breathes, finding his release.

Easing my ass back onto the edge of the sink, he leans against me. Grazing my fingertips to the curve of his hips, I pull him closer as his cum leaks down my thigh.

"Now *that*, little Quinn—" He firmly takes my jaw in his hand, tracing my lips with his thumb. "*That* is how you deserve to be fucked. Always."

CHAPTER FIVE

Music erupts from the speakers, vibrations flowing through the bodies in motion. The flashing strobe lights and smoke creeping its way up from the floor create a seductive ambiance, the living room being the most crowded area of the party. Black and orange balloons blanket the ceiling, a giant hanging spider decoration draped over our heads.

The energy and atmosphere are intense, and everyone seems to be having the time of their lives. And for once, I'm finally *living*, and having the time of *my* life.

I've never been one to let loose. I've always lived my life in a bubble, keeping myself distanced from everyone. I guess it's safe to say that has always been my coping skill.

That's how I've learned to protect myself, since nobody else ever has. Yet, tonight, I'm finally letting go, embracing the endless possibilities.

Swaying my hips and dancing to the beat, I sing along to the lyrics. Stretching out my arms above my head, and moving to the rhythm, the Halloween punch and gelatin shot from earlier begin to creep up on me.

The *Monster Mash* begins to play, and everyone feels the vibe. Allowing my eyes to scan the room, I finally spot my three protectors leaning against the wall. Their attention is set on me, and *only* me, as they silently observe my every move.

Grazing my hands over my body, I start at my chest, slowly trailing down my abdomen, hips, and thighs. Seductively staring in their direction, not having a single care in the world.

Jason and Michael's backs are pressed to the wall, arms folded over their chest. Ghost's posture stiffens, his arms dropping to the sides as his hands ball into tight fists.

Confusion strikes me until I feel a light tap on my shoulder.

Turning around, I take in the sight of a guy dressed in black pants and a white T-shirt smeared with fake blood.

He smiles, dancing his way closer to me. "Loving the costume," he says over the music.

"Thanks," I reply, swaying my hips to the beat. "I have no idea what I'm supposed to be, though—"

He unexpectedly grabs onto my waist, pulling me close. "You're hot as hell."

"Thanks," I reply uneasily, pulling away.

He grabs my wrist, bringing me back to him, and locks me

in place. "Where you going?"

"You're hurting me," I stammer.

Ghost appears, stepping between us. "Get your fucking hands off her."

"Or what?"

He lifts his knife and spins it between his fingers. "Or I'll gut you like a fish," he coldly remarks.

My heart immediately sinks.

"Ghost," I try to say, but there's barely any sound to my voice.

Finally, he releases me, only to get right in Ghost's face. "Let her decide who she wants," he snaps back. "She's not your bitch."

Without warning, Ghost shoves him hard enough to send him flying backward. The moment his back collides with the wall, he lifts his hands above his head in defeat.

But it's already too late.

Ghost grabs his wrist, pinning his arm to the wall. It takes me a moment to realize what has just happened before I'm able to snap back to reality. There's a knife stuck through his palm. The blade is buried through his flesh, locking him in place, blood seeping down his arm from the gash.

There's a high-pitched ringing in my ears. My eyes nearly bulge out of my head in disbelief. And then the ringing fades, and he's screaming.

Screaming in agony and fear.

My stomach turns. Adrenaline pumps through me.

Ghost screams back, mocking him. "If you ever put your filthy hands on what's mine again, I will hunt you down, and I will kill you. Slowly."

He twists the knife, blood spurting out from around the incision of the blade, and there's a bloodcurdling scream. Everyone in the room is shrieking, cowering, and staying out of the way as Ghost withdraws the knife from his flesh.

Dropping to his knees, he cradles his injured hand against his chest, hunched over in distress. Now his white T-shirt is stained with real blood.

How festive.

Ghost and Jason lead the way as we head toward the back door, while Michael walks beside me, glancing down at me occasionally to ensure I'm okay. All eyes are on us as we exit the party, taking our time cutting through the backyard and past everyone who's gathered outside.

Michael pulls out his phone, turning on the flashlight the moment we enter the woods. Ten minutes of walking must pass before we finally reach the main road, and I come to realize we're right near downtown Salem.

There's a crowd of people walking in the middle of the street in every direction, all dressed in costumes, and the roads are blocked off with police vehicles, barriers, and orange cones. After taking a turn and walking down a side street, the back heels of my feet are blistered and throbbing.

Slowing my pace, I try to take my mind off the discomfort, although it's useless. Kneeling, I untie my heels and pull them off, holding onto Michael's arm to keep myself steady.

"You good?" Jason asks.

Nodding slightly, I hold onto my heels and continue to follow behind them. "I'm fine," I say, sharp pebbles from the concrete jabbing the soles of my feet. I wince.

"Give me them," Jason says, taking my heels.

Ghost stands in front of me, blocking my path as I come

to a stop. Before I can even make sense of it, he lifts me from the ground and scoops me into his arms as if I weigh nothing.

"You don't need to carry me," I rush out, taken aback. "I can walk. Really."

"I want you against me," he breathes.

"You keep protecting me. Why?"

"I see right through you."

Frowning, I shake my head. "What does that even mean?"

"It's all you've ever wanted. To be protected. Safe," he sharply states, cutting across the front lawn of a house. "We will keep you safe, little Quinn."

My heart hammers, and my stomach flutters. *Butterflies.*

"As crazy as this is, that was really sweet," I murmur.

The four of us make our way up the front steps, crossing the porch and coming to a halt as we reach the front door.

"I didn't come to your rescue because I'm your knight in shining armor." He places me onto my feet, before taking my face between his gloved hands. "I'm the villain, and I want you all to myself."

The front door creaks open, darkness welcoming us.

My heart accelerates, drumming wildly. Goosebumps rise on my skin.

Dropping his arms to his sides, he steps back. Jason and Michael enter the home, and are swallowed by the darkness, leaving the door wide open behind them.

Ghost slowly pulls down the hood of his costume, grips the bottom of his mask, and pulls it over his head. And finally, after all night, he's *unmasked.*

The dim porch light is bright enough to bring out his

striking blue eyes, surrounded by thick, dark lashes, highlighting his disheveled, black hair. He wets his plump lips with the tip of his tongue before they curl into a devious smirk. His sharp, chiseled jawline clenches tight, as my gaze travels down to the tattoos covering his neck. Ghost is more handsome than I ever could have fathomed, which only seems to make this harder.

And he looks so familiar, yet I can't seem to place him.

Swallowing hard, I anxiously blink up at him. "I've seen you before."

His face hardens. "Have you?"

"Yes."

Cocking his head to the side, he sadistically grins. "Are you sure?" he challenges.

"I didn't think you were ever going to take your mask off."

"I didn't plan on it," he confesses, dropping his gaze to my lips. "But then how could I do this?"

Within seconds, he's pulling me closer, and pressing his mouth against mine. He kisses me hard, aggressively holding me against him. My body dissolves against his, sparks flying. The tip of his tongue traces the seam of my lips, begging for entrance, and I eagerly grant it.

Our tongues brush together, impatiently, and he takes full control. Moving me backward, he pins me to the wall beside the front door, grazing his hands over every curve of my body. Catching his groan in my mouth, my breathing quickens, and the brisk, autumn air sends a shiver down my spine.

Ghost caresses my bare arms, warming me with the friction from his gloves. He leans into me, taking my bottom lip between his teeth. I moan in utter satisfaction, reaching up to lock my arms around his neck. Breathing in his heady cologne, an ache settles between my legs, before he bends down and lifts me effortlessly from the ground.

"Fuck," he breathes, returning his now raw, red lips to mine.

Running my fingers through his slick hair, I melt into him, pushing my lower half against the large bulge in his pants. I've never been kissed like this in my life.

Drawing back his head, he rests his forehead against mine, and stares straight into my soul. "I plan on fucking you both violently, and passionately, all night long," he coldly warns, eyes narrowed. "I'm giving you ten seconds to leave."

"What?" I nearly whisper.

Placing me back onto my bare feet, he moves away, his demeanor drastically changing. "If you're not gone in ten seconds, then your decision has been made."

"The night isn't over."

"Ten," he begins.

"We had a deal," I press.

"Nine."

"I asked you to bring my darkest fantasies to life."

"Eight," he tests.

"I want this," I admit, more to myself than to him.

"Seven."

"I want you."

"Six," he sharply exhales. "Five. Four."

"I'm not changing my mind," I boldly tell him.

"Three…"

"Two," I taunt.

Suddenly, he becomes silent. Allowing me a final moment

to change my mind. To run. I don't move an inch.

And his eyes narrow. "*One.*"

CHAPTER SIX

The seductive, slow melody I've just chosen sounds through the Bluetooth speaker in the living room of their apartment. Ghost hands me a glass of the energy drink and vodka mixture I had requested as Jason sits beside me on the black leather couch.

Sexual tensions couldn't be higher.

He reaches behind his shoulder and pulls the robe of his costume over his head, leaving him in a black tank and pants. My mouth falls open as I take in the sight of his heavily tattooed and defined arms, shoulders, and neck—all rippling with veins and muscle.

Jason grabs the bottle of whiskey from Michael, who shortly dismisses himself from the room. Pouring himself a glass, Jason slightly lifts the bottom of his mask, revealing the lower half of his face. Pouty pink lips press against the glass as he swallows down the strong liquor with one gulp.

Ghost sits beside me, locking me between the two of them. "What's next, little Quinn?" he asks with a crooked grin. "What are some of those dark fantasies of yours?"

Taking a sip of my drink, I squirm in my seat. "I'm not sure," I reply.

"Don't be afraid," he purrs, gripping my leg right above my knee. His hand is huge compared to my thigh. "Tonight, we will give you everything you crave and *more*."

"We," I echo, uncertain.

"If that's what you want," he begins, sensually grazing his fingers along my inner thigh. "Then that's what you'll get."

"I've only ever read about this," I sheepishly admit. "It's always been just a fantasy."

"You asked me to bring them to life," Ghost urges. "Are you taking that back?"

"No," I rush out. "I told you I want this."

Jason takes the glass from my hand—startling me—before setting it onto the table. Returning his attention to me, he leans against the backrest of the couch, placing his hand on my other leg.

Ghost grips my neck, and when I tilt my head back in submission, he smiles deviously. Those pearly white teeth make me weak. Bringing me closer, he presses his lips to my neck, as I allow my eyes to flutter shut, taking in the eroticism of this moment.

Both men caress up and down my legs. An electrical

current is in the air, and I'm not only drawn to Ghost, but to Jason as well.

His lips are soft and warm, causing goosebumps to rise on my skin. He licks, sucks, and bites his way down to my collarbone. Arching my back, wetness pools between my thighs. I am drenched for them.

Placing my hand over Jason's, I guide him between my legs, hesitating at the buttons of my bodysuit. His groan is deep, sending tingles throughout my body. My mouth falls open in ecstasy as I give in to the incredible sensations of Ghost's lips trailing up my neck, his warm breath fanning the delicate skin beneath my ear.

Jason kneels on the floor directly in front of me, spreads my legs, and moves me to the edge of the couch. Readjusting his mask to the top of his head, he buries his face between my thighs and takes me into his mouth.

Letting out a soft moan, I'm already so close to getting off from the excitement alone. Ghost holds my throat, tightening his grip, as Jason quickly flicks his tongue against my clit in the most perfect motion and rhythm.

Thrusting his finger inside of me, he flattens his tongue and twirls in precise circles, sending every nerve ending into overdrive. My inner walls tighten, spasming around him, before he adds in another, fucking me savagely with long, slippery fingers.

"I envy him right now," Ghost breathes beside my ear, applying more pressure to my throat, making it hard to breathe. "That sweet little pussy is my favorite meal."

My climax claims me without warning. Jason sucks my clit, lightly grazing his teeth on my sensitive flesh. Grabbing the back of his head, I pull him closer, grinding myself against his face. He withdraws his fingers from my wetness and wraps his arms under my legs, gripping my thighs.

Pulling me closer, he devours me, making me come so intensely it's almost painful. Moaning loudly, I squirm against his mouth, bucking my hips and arching my back even more. Letting out helpless, little cries of overwhelming pleasure with each passing second.

"Fuck," Jason grunts, shrugging off his bulky jacket.

He reaches down, lifting me into his arms bridal style. My arms find their way around his neck, and finally, I'm able to see his face. My heart instantly hammers at how drop-dead gorgeous he is. Dark brown hair and hazel eyes, with such masculine facial features.

How did I manage to get so lucky tonight?

Pushing a door open with his shoulder, he walks us into a room, pressing my back to the bed. Reaching behind him, he pulls his shirt over his head, revealing large tattoos on his arms, chest, and ribs. He crawls onto me, the toned frame of his chest pressed to mine.

And he stares at my mouth. "Do you want to taste yourself?"

"Yes," I whisper.

He stares hungrily into my eyes, and with a quiet groan, he presses his lips to mine. Pushing his tongue into my mouth, forcefully. Greedily. Leaning one forearm beside my head, he reaches down with his hand, taking mine and guiding it to the large and hard bulge beneath his pants.

Pulling down his zipper, my fingers fumble at the button until he swats me away. Ripping it open impatiently, he pulls his pants down just enough, and his long, thick cock springs free.

Rubbing the smooth, rosy head up and down the wet slit of my sex, his lips leave mine, cascading down my neck. Jason buries himself inside of me with one long stroke. It takes my breath away, as he stretches me wide, thrusting into my wetness again and again.

My nails dig into his back, as he drives into me hard, increasing his pace. He lifts my leg over his hip, granting him more access. My body accepts him deeper, inch after inch, his engorged cock hitting all the right places.

His breathing becomes labored as he pounds into me, a strangled whimper escaping my wide opened mouth. Grabbing my jaw, he turns my head to the side, where I spot Ghost standing in the doorway.

Staring straight at me. Watching us.

Jason reaches down between my legs, rubbing his thumb over my clit in slow, torturous circles. My legs start shaking, before tightly locking around his waist. Sneaking his arm under my back, he flips us over until I'm straddling him.

Ghost climbs onto the bed behind me, gripping the back of my neck and pushing me forward, lifting my ass higher.

"I want you," I tell him. "I want you both."

"I know, baby," he grunts, lubing my back entrance with cold gel. "We'll take care of you. Deep breaths."

Inhaling a small breath, my eyes close as I begin to ride Jason. Slow, steady movements, as Ghost eases his fingers into my ass. Stretching me, working me, curling his fingers in just the right spot before removing them altogether.

The tip of his cock circles over my back entrance, while Jason is nuzzled in my cunt. Taking his time, Ghost eases into my ass, and it feels as if I'm being split in half. Inch by inch, he sinks into me further, until he's buried to the hilt.

Ghost and Jason both fill me, and I'm already there.

Pressing my face into Jason's shoulder, he secures his arms around my waist, lifting his hips to pound into me. Ghost sinks into my ass repeatedly, firmly smacking my cheeks with each thrust. I have never felt anything this powerful, and I have never felt so consumed.

My orgasm bursts through me, overtaking my entire body, wave after wave.

"There's no escape, baby," Ghost says, slamming into my ass, over and over.

"You fell into our trap," Jason groans beside my ear, grazing his teeth on my shoulder. "We're never letting you go."

"*Scream for us*," Ghost commands.

"Oh, yes," I whimper, convulsing against their solid bodies, screaming. "Oh, God, yes!"

"Your tight little ass feels so good around my cock," Ghost grunts, plunging deeper.

Harder.

Faster.

"Choke me," I moan out, pleading.

"She's a good girl," Jason praises, wrapping his fingers around my throat, applying just enough pressure to make me see tiny spots of white light. "Aren't you?"

"Such a good fucking girl," Ghost groans, his breathing shallow as he thrusts into my ass ruthlessly, tugging hard on my hair. "Fuck. So *tight*. You're doing such a good job taking us."

"Yes, baby," Jason grunts, bucking his hips from the mattress, drilling into me. "I'm going to fill you up."

He tightens his hold on my throat, and another orgasm rips through me. Riding out this everlasting euphoria, I'm suddenly seeing stars through my eyelids. The pressure on my throat cutting off my air supply only seems to make me climax even harder. Milking them dry, they both fill me with their cum.

Just as I'm about to fade away, Jason takes my face between his hands, bringing me back. My eyes flutter open, and his eyes are like daggers, piercing through me.

"You good?" he questions, caressing my cheekbone with his thumb.

"Yes," I whisper, my voice hoarse. "Better than good."

They both pull out of me, and their cum drips down my inner thighs. As I roll over and lay on my back between them, my breathing hitches.

Ghost stands, completely naked, and absolutely covered in tattoos. He grabs a folded towel from the corner of the room and wipes me dry, cleaning up the mess they made between my legs. Tossing it onto the hardwood floor, he pulls on his pants until he becomes still.

Completely motionless.

And within seconds, I finally realize what he's staring down at.

The healed scars on my wrists.

CHAPTER SEVEN

Quickly sitting upright, I rush to my feet. Fastening the buttons of my bodysuit, an eerie silence takes over the room. When I turn to face them, they're gaping at me.

"It's not polite to stare," I tell them.

Ghost approaches me, taking my shoulders in his hands. "In the bathroom, earlier," he hesitates, and my stomach sinks. "At the party. You were upset. Who was that girl?"

"She was nobody," I reply, brushing it off. "It's really not a big deal."

"I can see right through you, little Quinn."

"Why are you asking?"

"Because you're hurting. And I don't ever want to see you hurt."

Holding up my wrists, I gaze down at the scars, memories flooding back to me. I've never had anyone to talk to about this. Not ever. As strange as it may be, it's consoling that they want me to share my darkest secrets.

Staring into his eyes, I release a small breath. "My childhood sucked and school was even worse. I was bullied." I force a laugh. "Really, *really* bad."

"I'm sorry," he mutters, bringing me into his warm, bare chest. "I'll kill them."

"It's been a few years," I say dryly. "But... the trauma it caused. The second-guessing. Wondering if maybe, the whole time, they were right."

He pulls back, taking my face between his hands. "Right about what?"

"They told me it was my fault that my dad killed himself," I softly say, tears springing to my eyes.

His body tenses. Face hardens. And those *eyes*.

They're terrifying.

Anger consumes every ounce of his being.

Turning to Jason, he glares at him. It's evident that they're silently exchanging words before Ghost releases me and storms out of the room.

"These bullies," Jason says, now dressed, as he tucks a strand of hair behind my ear. "Do they live around here?"

"I'm not sure," I quietly reply. "But they all work at the haunted house every year."

"The one here in Salem?"

I nod.

"You know it's not true," he urges, brushing my face with his fingertips. "Right?"

My body stiffens, as I draw in a shaky breath.

"Quinn," Jason presses, frowning. "You know that was bullshit, right?"

"Mhm," I whisper.

"It was a bullshit fucking lie. There is no truth in that," he tells me. "Have you ever talked to anyone about this?"

"No."

"Why?"

"I didn't want to cause my mom any more stress," I admit, my lips quivering. "She's been through enough. I didn't want to be another burden in her life—"

"Stop," Jason stops me, wiping away a tear with his thumb. "You're not a burden."

"Don't you fret, little Quinn," Ghost says as he enters the room. "They're going to pay for what they did to you." He steps between Jason and me, pressing a lingering kiss on my forehead. "They're going to pay with their life."

The motorcycle engines roar as we speed down the street. The brisk night air sends goosebumps all over my body. Wrapping my arms tighter around Ghost's waist, he grips just above my knee with his hand, comforting me.

I melt against him.

It must look so crazy seeing men on bikes in costume, wearing Halloween masks as we drive past. We pull onto a dark and quiet road, the only light coming from the headlights of their motorcycles. It's an eerie scene as we turn into an empty lot, surrounded by woods.

The engines go silent, and suddenly I'm able to hear the faint sounds of Halloween-themed music in the distance. The tune of the *Michael Myers* theme song.

"Just for you, Mike," Ghost says to Michael, before helping me off his bike and removing my helmet for me, draping it over a handlebar.

"Where are we?" I ask, over the sound of the buzzing insects and leaves rustling on the ground from the wind.

"Back entrance," Jason smugly answers, reminding me of earlier.

"We're at the haunt?"

"Don't you want to have some real fun?" Ghost asks, adjusting his mask. "Let's pay your bullies a visit. It's time for revenge."

"I don't want them to see me," I stutter, uneasily, following behind them as we enter the dark wooded area.

"You don't have to, baby," Ghost coos, linking his gloved fingers through mine. "Leave that part to us."

Michael leads the way with his flashlight. The music grows louder with each passing minute. The atmosphere is frightening, exhilarating, as the screams from guests echo through the night air. Entering a cornfield, my three protectors march toward the side entrance to the haunted house in the distance.

Coming across a group of four, we stand silently behind the trees, watching the glow sticks glow brighter and brighter as they approach us.

Michael steps out, getting a bloodcurdling shriek out of them as they run up the path. Jason laughs at the encounter, yet Ghost remains silent.

Completely on edge. Boiling with rage.

"What are you going to do?" I ask him, staring into the dark eyes of his mask.

"I'm going to scare them," he responds coldly. "I want to see the fear in their eyes."

Jason slows his pace, facing us as he walks backward. "How many?" he questions, his business-like tone sending a shiver down my spine.

"They all work in the haunted house," I anxiously reply. "Every single one of them."

"That's a lot of people," Jason mutters.

"It's fine," Ghost dismisses. As we come to a halt, he gazes down at me. "I need names."

"Names?" I ask.

"Name the ones who were the worst," he orders. "The ones who really hurt you."

Memories come flashing back to me, as I take a moment to ponder my response. This one isn't hard. It's easy.

"The guys were the worst," I answer carefully. "Derek. John. And Alex."

"Good girl," he breathes, caressing my face. "Do you want to watch, little Quinn?"

My heart pounds as I slowly shake my head.

"Okay," he whispers. "Then you stay right here. Don't move. No matter what you hear, or see, do not move from this spot."

"Okay," I whisper back.

And they stalk toward the house.

CHAPTER EIGHT

GHOST POV

"Block the front entrance," I instruct Michael, pure hatred boiling inside of me, determined to break free in a form of utter chaos. "Jason, you cover the exit. Text me when the last group of people is out."

"On it," Jason says, disappearing around the side of the house.

Michael moves to the top step, blocking the way.

"Nobody in," I bite out, seeing red. "And nobody *out*."

Stepping inside, there's a gloomy, gray vibe. The windows are heavily boarded up, the wooden floor creaks beneath my boots, and the music grows louder. Scanning the dimly lit hallway, nobody is in sight. Even through my mask, this place wreaks of gasoline from nearby machinery and damp wood.

My phone buzzes in my pocket.

Jason

Last group is out

Removing the knife from the back of my waistline, I turn the corner.

"Derek," I call out, taunting him, tracing the blade with the tip of my fingers, as adrenaline pumps through me.

"Yeah, bro," he calls backs almost immediately. "Who's that?"

"Come find out."

He steps out from behind a fake wall, dressed in his stupid little costume. "Sick Ghostface mask," he observes, laughing. "Do I know you?"

Stalking toward him, my grip tightens on the handle of my knife. "Not quite," I answer. "I'm a friend of Quinn's."

Confusion claims his face as he moves beside the dim light plastered to the wall. "Quinn?" he asks.

Impatiently cocking my head to the side, I nod. "Ring any bells?"

"Oh. Yeah. That weird little bitch whose dad offed himself, right?"

Tossing him against the wall of the hallway, I waste no time in jabbing my knife into his chest. There's blood spurting, bones crunching. Over and over, and over again, I gut him, painting the walls, floors, and my mask in red. He chokes on his own blood, gurgling, half-sobbing for me to put an end to my vicious attack.

There's no stopping now.

I made a promise to my little Quinn that I would make them pay. With their life.

Their blood.

His body becomes limp against the wall. Yanking the blade from his ribcage, Derek lifelessly drops to the floor with a hard *thud*.

One down.

The rest to go.

Adrenaline rages through me as I rush into another room, spotting a guy in scene, dressed as a crazy, old scientist. How fucking cliché.

"Are you going to be my next subject?" he asks, reciting his corny line, gesturing down to a fake corpse on what appears to be a metal operating table.

"No," I growl, jumping over the table as he stumbles backward. "But you're mine."

He turns to run from me, shocked and confused, until I bury my knife into his back. Crippling over, he then drops to his knees, in a state of shock. That's when the pain finally hits him, ripping through his body. And he screams in both agony and fear, as I twist the blade sideways in his flesh.

"John?" I sadistically ask, demanding an answer.

"Y-y-yes," he chokes out, collapsing onto the floor, convulsing.

"Johnny boy!" I humorously shout, yanking out the knife before rolling up my sleeves.

With a quick toss in the air, I catch my knife by the rippled handle, before burying the sharp metal between his shoulder blades next.

"This is for Quinn," I mutter dryly, kicking him in the ribs. "One stab for every year you and your friends tortured her."

There's another *crunch* as I stab him again. Again. And again. I end up getting off track and lose count in a fit of rage. There's more gurgling. Quiet whimpers of desperation, as he begins to crawl forward, using what little energy he has left.

"How aren't you dead yet?" I joke, stepping on his back, now covered with deep gashes, and soaked with blood. I click my tongue at him. "You're not going anywhere, Johnny boy. This is the part where you die for what you did to her."

And right on cue, any hint of remaining life leaves his body.

Jason enters the room, catching me off guard, his jacket stained with blood. "There's gasoline out back in a shed."

"Good find," I sharply breathe, pulling my knife from Johnny boy's flesh.

"I grabbed some and left it at the back door."

"Where's Alex?" I demand, still fuming.

With a nod of his head, he motions to another hallway.

There he is in the center of the room, chained to a wooden chair, duct tape covering his mouth. My dick twitches at the thought of ending his life.

Getting revenge for little Quinn.

It's a sight to see as tears stream down his face.

"*Poor Alex*," I recite Ghostface's famous line. "You think this is all about you? You think you're still the star?"

He mumbles against the tape, until I rip it off. "What the

fuck is this," he squeals, desperation and fear flickering in his eyes.

"This is about Quinn. What you did to her," I spit out.

"You're fucking crazy," he shrieks.

"Crazy for her," I say through clenched teeth, ripping off my mask, and shoving my face in his. "You fucked up. And now, you're going to pay for it."

"Help," he shouts, becoming silent as I press the tip of my blade against his neck.

"Your friends can't help you," I shout back, cutting his throat. "They're dead."

A girl rushes into the room and screams out in horror, taking in the sight of blood pouring from the gaping slit. Jason chases after her into another room, disappearing from my view.

Pulling on my mask, I grab the gasoline at the back door. Jason enters through a doorway shortly after, tossing a bloody, metal bat onto the ground.

"Start at the front," I instruct, handing him the canister of gasoline.

"What if we missed someone?" he asks.

"The flames will take care of the others."

He nods, exiting the room.

"Ghost?"

My gaze darts over to the soft voice coming from the back door, when suddenly, I see her. *Quinn.*

"What are you doing here?" I harshly question.

"I was worried," she fearfully replies, stepping into the room. "I needed to make sure you were alright."

Stepping toward her, she moves back, until her body is

trapped against the wall. My cock swells, uncomfortably straining against my pants.

"Fuck," I grunt, slamming my hands onto the wall beside her head, locking her between my arms.

A sexy, little squeal escapes her lips.

"You make my dick so fucking hard, Quinn, it hurts," I groan, leaning against her.

All this murder has really gotten to me this time. The sight of blood always makes my dick hard. I *need* to be inside her. Buried in that tight, wet, little cunt.

"I need to fuck you," I breathe, throwing back my head as she unbuttons my pants. "Right now."

Dropping to her knees, she yanks down my pants, and wastes no time wrapping her lips around my cock. Thrusting forward, she gags, while I plunge in and out of her warm mouth. Firmly holding myself at the base with my forefinger and thumb, I guide her hand to my balls.

"Oh, fuck, baby," I grunt with each thrust.

She gags on my dick again, her cheeks flushing, tears leaking from the corners of her eyes. She's trying to please me with everything in her.

And she does.

Leaning down, I link my arm around her and ease her onto her back, pinning her to the dusty hardwood floor. After tearing open the buttons at her crotch, I spit in my hand, burying it between her thighs to get her ready for me.

But she is already drenched with her own juices.

I waste no time driving into her, as her pussy sucks at my cock with each thrust. She feels so good. *Too* fucking good. She's my new obsession and she doesn't have the slightest clue.

"Yes," she whimpers, fisting the robe over my chest. "Yes, daddy, yes!"

As soon as *daddy* leaves her lips, I drill into her faster, locking my fingers around her throat. Taking her breath away. Fucking her without emotion. Without remorse.

Just deep, forceful strokes as her body stiffens beneath me.

Slamming into her, again and again, I fuck her violently, just as I had promised.

Withdrawing the knife from the sheath at the back of my pants, I press the tip to her throat. She gasps, squirming beneath me.

"Yes," she encourages, and that's all I need. "Please."

Dragging the tip of the blade down her neck, I lightly nick her collarbone, and her body reacts with a shudder. Moaning for me, Quinn tilts her head to the side, exposing her throat. Sinking my cock inside of her slowly, I graze the blade to the sensitive flesh beneath her ear, smearing blood on her skin.

"Oh, God," she cries, bucking her hips, matching my strokes. "Oh, *God.*"

"God isn't here right now," I confirm, nicking her skin again.

Again.

And *again*.

Suddenly, smoke pours into the room, and the smell of gasoline becomes overwhelming. Flames erupt around us, starting off small, and then growing larger. Quinn stares up at me with fear, unsettled, as I continue to fuck her mercilessly.

"Ghost," she chokes out.

"You're safe. Take off my mask, baby," I instruct, and she listens. "That's my good girl. Now put it on."

And she obeys again, pulling the Ghostface mask over her head.

Halloween-themed music roars through the house, as the smoke thickens, and the bright light from the flames intensifies. Agonizing screams from the fear and pain of being trapped in the house and burned alive echo through the halls.

My body is thick with sweat from the intense heat. I make sure to keep my attention on the raging fire, which creeps its way across the ceiling, burning the wood structures. Slamming into her, I drop the knife, lifting her leg over my hip so she can take me deeper. And she comes for me, gripping my dick tight, her innocent little cries stifled from the mask.

"Fuck, baby," I groan, entering her harder.

And I find my release with her, lungs burning, choking, and grunting with each stroke, now surrounded by a blanket of smoke.

Seeing nothing but *black*.

Fuck. Fuck. Fuck.

Scooping her into my arms, and holding her tight, I bolt through the doorway exiting the house. I carry her outside, where we can finally breathe, my dick still hanging out of my pants.

All that matters is *her*.

Her safety.

Michael and Jason race toward us, as I drop to my knees and lay her on the grass, the house bursting into flames behind us. Windows explode and glass shatters. Police and fire engine sirens roar in the distance. Yanking the mask over her head, my heart hammers against my ribcage at the thought of losing her.

"Quinn," I urge, lightly smacking her face.

"Ouch," she murmurs, and a smile plays at the corner of her lips. "What was that for?"

Sharply exhaling, I shake my head at her in disbelief.

"I'm okay, Ghost," she whispers, gently cupping my face with her hand. The vulnerability that washes over me from her touch catches me completely off guard. "I'm safe with you."

Yeah, you are, little Quinn.

More than you know.

CHAPTER NINE

The night air sends a cold shiver through me. All I can hear is the sound of my teeth clattering together and burning wood. I can see my own breath. The four of us enter the woods, and the flames from the haunted house are so bright, they somehow manage to light our way out. The sirens grow louder, coming from behind us, and people are shouting in distress.

Rubbing my arms, trying to warm myself, I realize it's no use. Ghost removes the robe of his costume and pulls it over my head. Shrugging into the sleeves, I snuggle into the warmth, breathing in the heady, intoxicating scent of his cologne.

There's a mix of musk and *copper*.

Shivering from the icy breeze, I gaze apologetically into his eyes. "Aren't you cold now?"

"I'm fine," he counters.

"How?" I gasp, looking over his defined forearms.

I finally notice the *blood*.

Yet he says nothing as he pulls up the hood, covering my head, protecting my numb ears from the harsh wind.

Scurrying to the excluded area where they parked their motorcycles, Ghost faces me, placing the helmet onto my head. He fastens the buckle beneath my jaw before straddling his bike, kicking back the stand.

Gripping his shoulder, ready to climb on behind him, he stops me.

"You're riding with Michael, baby," he announces.

I frown, confusion washing over me. "Oh?"

"Better to be cautious, little Quinn," Ghost explains, pulling on his blood-spattered mask.

"Hop on," Michael instructs, offering his hand.

Placing my hand in his, I climb on behind him, locking my arms around his waist. He's huge compared to me. His body is as hard as stone, and suddenly I wonder what it looks like beneath the jumpsuit of his costume.

A dull ache settles between my legs at the thought of having three of them.

Ghost nods, and within seconds, the engines roar to life, echoing through the woods. Unexpectedly, flashlights shine in our direction, and the leaves begin to rustle on the dirt ground. It's clear we are no longer alone.

"Hey!" a man shouts loudly. "This is the police. Hands where I can see them!"

"Now," Ghost snaps. All three of us take off, pulling off to the right. The tires screech as we speed down the road.

"Stop right there!"

We faintly hear another police officer shouting commands, until the sound of his voice is drowned out from the loud revving of the motorcycles. My heart races, adrenaline coursing through me. All my senses become heightened as I grip Michael tighter, burying my face into his back.

Sirens wail, drawing in on us. Flashing lights from police cars pull out further down the road. They're headed straight toward us.

Ghost immediately slows down, and holds his arm out to the side, gesturing for us to hang a hard left turn down an abandoned side street.

"Get her out of here," he shouts.

Michael makes a sharp turn, and my heart sinks.

"Wait," I squeal, realizing that Ghost and Jason are not planning on accompanying us. "Wait!" I scream, glancing back, only to notice they're already gone.

They're headed straight for the police.

"What the fuck are they doing?" I plead to Michael, hugging him tighter.

"Don't worry about them," he consoles me. "They'll be fine."

"But how do you know that—"

Tightly gripping my knee, he caresses my skin. "It's a distraction," he explains, racing down the long, narrow road. "They know what they're doing."

"They do?"

He nods in response.

"Okay," I weakly say, doubting him.

"Is this your first time running from the cops?" he asks, nonchalantly.

"Yes," I admit. "Why?"

Then it hits me.

It's not *their* first time. From his eerie silence, he makes it clear that it won't be the last.

Anxiously pacing across the living room of their apartment, negative thoughts and images flood through my mind. Worst-case scenarios. I am a complete and utter wreck, terrified of the unknown. Paranoia has me by the throat.

It's a gut-wrenching feeling that I'm no stranger to.

The house is silent. All I can hear is a high-pitched ringing in my ears, along with the sound of Michael's boots creeping up beside me. Releasing a deep breath, I nervously chew on my nails.

Walking up and down the hall, again and again, I try desperately to keep myself calm and collected. But it's been too long. Something just isn't right. I can't help the feeling of guilt that eats away at me with each passing second.

"It's my fault," I murmur, finally breaking my silence. "This is all my fault."

"No," Michael replies abruptly, spinning me around to face him, gripping me hard. "That's not true."

"You guys went there to get revenge for me," I point out, gazing up at his cold, blank mask. "If it wasn't for me, then we never would have gone there. Then maybe the police wouldn't have assumed that we somehow started the fire. I mean, that's why they tried stopping us from leaving, right? Because they thought it was us?"

He remains silent.

Frowning, I gawk at him in horror. "Was it us?"

He continues to say nothing.

"I just hope everyone got out in time," I say, more to myself than to him.

Without warning, he removes his mask. For the first time tonight, I see his face. He's so brutally handsome. *Strikingly* handsome, with sharp, masculine features. Brown eyes surrounded by thick, dark lashes that turn me to mush. Blond, messy hair that's loosely tied back.

He steps forward, towering over my small frame, forcing me backward until I'm trapped against the wall. "You're safe," he whispers, sending me into a trance. "Breathe."

Inhaling a shaky breath through my nose, my body finally begins to relax.

"That's it," he urges, taking my hand and placing it onto my chest. "*Breathe.*"

Again, I inhale a long breath, before slowly releasing it. The entire time, our eyes are locked in a captivating stare. There's just something about the monotone, yet soft sound of his voice, and the way he soothes me.

There's an endless depth behind his gaze, except he's unreadable.

Empty.

I'm hypnotized. Locked in place. Unable to move.

To *think*.

"Good girl," he praises, leaning into me. "Again, Quinn. *Breathe*."

My heart rate slows, and I allow my eyes to shut, giving in to the comforting sensations that consume me as his voice silences my intrusive thoughts. Time passes by, and then out of nowhere, the sound of the front door crashing open brings me back.

Ghost and Jason enter the house, unmasked, covered in blood, and I run to them. Relief consumes me as they pull me into a strong embrace, and I silently scold myself for caring so much. For feeling so much for them, so quickly.

Instead of questioning everything, and hating myself for letting them in, I chose to do the opposite.

I give in to the inevitable bliss of being theirs for the rest of the night.

Pressing myself against Ghost, I lift my hand to the back of his neck, guiding him down to me. He leans forward, pressing his lips firmly against mine. Breathing me in deeply, feverishly. Quietly groaning under his breath. Running his hands through my hair, pulling tight on the strands, the back of my skull throbbing with pain.

I can't seem to get enough.

After breaking our heated kiss, I turn to Jason, and he *knows*.

He kisses me hard, longingly. So much lust. Passion.

Michael spins me around, taking my jaw in a firm grasp. He presses his full lips to mine, aggressively gripping my hips, as he brings me against him. Slipping his tongue into my mouth, he fights for control, and he wins.

Melting into him, he lifts me from the floor and tosses

me over his shoulder. He walks us into a room, Ghost and Jason trailing close behind us, and then he lowers me onto the bed. Grabbing my ankles, he flips me onto my stomach, tearing open the buttons at my crotch.

Fisting the sheets, the weight of his bare body leans against my backside, and he rubs the smooth tip of his cock up and down my wet slit. Michael enters me hard, and I take him all at once, stifling a cry into the mattress.

Barely giving me the chance to adjust to his invasion, he slams into me aggressively. Gripping the back of my neck, he pins me down, keeping me still. Stretching me wide, he plunges himself as deep as I can take him, breathing shallow with each forceful thrust.

"Fuck," he grunts, wrapping my hair around his wrist, and pulling tight.

Flipping me onto my back, he pulls me to the edge of the bed, and my legs spread for him on their own accord. He enters me slowly, before slamming into me hard. Over and over. Without mercy. Gripping my thighs, he digs his fingers into my skin.

Jason climbs onto the bed, working his thickness with his hand, before grazing the rosy head of his cock against my lips. Prying open my mouth with his thumb, he pushes himself into my mouth, my lips stretching wide around him. Cradling his shaft with my tongue, he fucks my mouth, fingers clasped tight around my throat.

A roar erupts from his chest, and his cock twitches. Licking the tip of his crown, I savor the taste of him, until he plunges himself into the back of my throat. Repeatedly. Gagging on his thickness, I bob my head, meeting his thrusts, while Michael continues his merciless strokes, grinding his hips against me.

"What are we going to do with you now, little Quinn?" Ghost sadistically questions, tossing a rope onto the bed beside us. "Tie her up."

Jason withdraws himself from my mouth, and secures the rope around my wrists, binding me tight. Reaching beneath my back, he holds me close, moving me further up the bed and pinning my entwined wrists over my head. The moment he secures the rope onto the hook built into the headboard, my eyes widen, flickering with anticipation.

Excitement.

Fear of the unknown.

"Look at our filthy little fuck toy," Jason purrs while I squirm on the bed eagerly,

yanking hard on the ropes. "You're so desperate to come. Aren't you, baby?"

I nod.

"Tell us," Ghost commands.

"Yes," I moan, and my legs fall open.

Michael tugs on his cock, working faster with a tight fist.

"Please," I eagerly whine, taking my bottom lip between my teeth.

"You want to be used by us, don't you?" Michael asks, inching closer, positioning himself between my thighs. I stare up at him dreamily before glancing over at Ghost and Jason.

"Yes," I plead. "Use me."

"What do you think?" Michael questions Jason, teasingly. "Do you think she can handle it?

Jason lightly caresses my knee with his hand before

spreading my legs wider, granting them every inch of me.

"I'm not so sure," Jason responds with a wicked grin. "I think it's time to test her."

"Mmm," Michael breathes, slight alarm igniting in my eyes. "He's right."

"But you've already fulfilled my darkest fantasies," I rush out.

Ghost releases a sadistic chuckle from beside the bed. "Oh, Quinn," he sighs, testing the

rope's hold on my delicate wrists, gazing down at my face with menacing eyes. "We'll show you dark."

I begin to squirm helplessly on the bed, my lips curling into a grin.

"You're not going anywhere," Jason taunts, retrieving a knife from the top of the nightstand before handing it to Michael.

Instantly, I freeze in place, staring at the sharp tip of the knife with uncertainty.

"What are you going to do to me?" I ask.

Ghost withdraws his own knife from the back of his pants, twirling it between his fingers skillfully while leaning over the bed. "We're going to fuck your pretty little cunt and tight ass with whatever we see fit," he bites out, burying his hand between my thighs and tracing my clit with his fingers.

I grind against his touch, moaning softly. "Ghost—"

A smile tugs at his lips. "And you're going to take it," he finishes, sinking two fingers deep inside me. "Aren't you, sweetheart?"

Without any hesitation, I nod. Suddenly, Michael is gazing

down at me, coating his fingers with lube and sinking one into my ass. "You are ours to play with," he groans.

"Our filthy little fuck toy," Jason breathes, placing a blindfold over my eyes. I can feel his fingertips lightly caressing the skin along my collarbone before curling them around my throat. "Ready to relinquish all power to us?"

A desperate cry escapes my lips.

"Surrender, Quinn," Ghost growls, fucking me harder with slippery fingers.

"Yes," I whimper, grinding my pussy and ass against their hands, taking them deeper.

"Say. It," Michael demands, curling his finger in my ass, stroking just the right spot.

My back bows. I tug hard on the ropes, giving in to the overwhelming yet incredible sensations. "I surrender," I gasp, breathlessly.

The smooth head of what must be Jason's cock traces my lips briefly, before I open my mouth wide, taking him all the way into the back of my throat. I bob my head, matching his urgent thrusts as my climax builds rapidly. I love being used by them. I can't seem to get enough. Something thicker is replaced with Ghost's fingers. Something... unfamiliar.

I cry out euphorically, humming with pleasure, my mouth still filled with Jason's cock and a thick film of saliva dripping down my chin. I'm so close to being swept away with my orgasm but I hold it back, which only seems to create more excitement. All four of us continue to fill the room with sharp breathing and moans.

Jason's thrusts become faster, and without warning, I explode around them, my back arching off the bed. The second I feel Michael's tongue on my clit, another wave of my orgasm hits me.

"Fuck," Jason groans, running his hands through my hair and pumping into my mouth faster. "Look at you, gagging on my thick cock. Such an eager little whore."

I gag violently from his size.

"God damn," he snarls.

"Gagged, blindfolded, and bound with ropes," Michael bites out.

"Fuck," Ghost snaps as his cell phone rings, removing whatever he has been thrusting inside me.

Michael traces his tongue up and down my pussy, when abruptly, something sharp drags along the skin over my hip, then slightly pressing into my thigh. A knife.

The realization finally hits me. The hilt of the knife was inside of me.

He dips his finger into the warm substance in the blade's wake and traces something small on my chest.

"I'm going to come," Jason sharply lets out. "And you're going to swallow every—" Thrust. "Last." Thrust. "Drop."

With that, he empties himself into the back of my throat.

"Mmm," I purr, licking my lips.

Michael thrusts inside of me with one hard stroke and comes immediately. My eyes flutter open as Jason removes the blindfold. My thigh is bleeding, and there's a tiny heart on my chest painted in blood.

I smile as they both collapse beside me.

CHAPTER TEN

Michael unties the rope from around my wrists, and my skin feels raw. All three of us lay together, sweaty, out of breath, and overtaken with bliss. Jason lightly strokes my forearm with his fingertips, while Michael's lips graze my shoulder. I've never felt so content, so fulfilled.

Michael reaches for the glass of water on his nightstand and offers it to me. "Drink," he says.

I do as I'm told, and the water immediately quenches my thirst. "Thank you," I say, grinning.

Michael smirks.

"Are you hungry?" Jason asks.

"Starving," I reply.

Pushing himself up from the bed, he retrieves his pants from the floor. "I'll go see what we have," he says, before leaving the room.

"Leftover pizza," Michael says, chugging the rest of the water.

I smile. "That sounds good."

"From a week ago," he adds.

"Even better," I laugh, until he slips his hand to the back of my neck, and his lips collide with mine.

My bare feet are quiet against the hardwood floor as I make my way into Ghost's room.

Darkness welcomes me, except for the faintest amount of light from the full moon shining in through the window. His bed is huge—king-size—and the ceiling is high. The walls are painted dark, and the space around us feels bare, until I notice a large bookshelf in the corner.

The sound of running water catches me off guard, and there's a bright light shining through the slight crack of another door from across the room. Peeking into the bathroom, I begin to second-guess myself, until the urge of needing to see him grows stronger.

The thin wall of glass from the shower showcases the perfect outline of his masculine frame. Steam and warmth take up the small space around us. Gently shutting the door behind me, sweat beads at the side of my head.

My clothes drop to the cold tile floor, pooling at my feet.

Sliding my fishnet stockings down my waist, thighs, and legs, I'm now completely naked.

Ghost sticks his head out of the shower, and his eyes widen with desire when he sees me. He stands there, fingers gripping the edge of the thin glass wall, completely motionless. A burning passion ignites in his eyes, and there's a magnetic pull between us, drawing us together.

"Get over here, little Quinn," he breathes sharply.

Taking me into his arms, he brings me into the shower, moving us under the stream of uncomfortably hot water. A dark, red substance drips from his disheveled hair, staining the water red at our feet, before it washes down the drain.

Blood. So much blood.

How did I not notice sooner? How was I so oblivious?

Placing a finger beneath my chin, he lifts my gaze from the blood-stained water, and my eyes meet his.

"You did this, for *me*," I weakly let out. "What did you do to them, Ghost?"

"Naïve, little Quinn. I'd sell my soul for you." Gripping my hips, he brings me close as his large, thick erection twitches against my stomach. "If I had one."

Leaning down, he brushes his lips on mine, taking my face between his rough hands. The heat from his body sends a shiver down my spine, and I lean into him, my fingertips grazing his chest. Resting my arms over his broad shoulders, my fingers glide through his wet hair, as his hands explore the curves of my ribs, hips, and lower back.

He catches my moan in his mouth, and his gentle touch turns to groping. He kisses me hard, demandingly. Moving me backward, he presses my back to the cold wall of the shower. He explores every inch of my body, leaving goosebumps in the wake of his fingertips.

His tongue pushes through the seam of my lips, and he explores my mouth hungrily. Breathing heavily. Cupping his large hands over my ass, he thrusts his hips against me. Stifling a moan at his lips, I grip his broad shoulders, pulling him closer, my breasts pressed firmly against his chest.

"Fuck," he moans, trailing his lips to my jaw, and down to my throat.

Ghost trails his hand up my spine, grasping the back of my neck, as he sucks, licks, and grazes his teeth on my sensitive flesh. He cups my breast with his hand, squeezing gently, tracing my nipple with his thumb.

He leans down, taking the puckered bud between his lips, and the warmth of his mouth almost brings me to my knees. Twirling and flicking my nipple with the tip of his tongue, he groans loudly against my skin, devouring me.

"God, yes," I whimper, running my fingers through his hair.

His cock is pulsating against me, twitching with satisfaction, as he kisses his way to the other side of my chest, where he returns the favor. My fingers graze down his toned abdomen, the lower V-shape at his hips, and I waste no time in locking my fingers around his cock.

He flinches, thrusting forward, slamming his palm against the wall to keep himself steady. Grinding into me, he fucks my hand, moaning loudly. His cock is so hard, it's absolutely throbbing for me. The desperation of needing to fill me flickers in his eyes.

"Please," he begs me, trembling. "I'm so goddamn hard." Again, he pushes forward into my grasp, grazing his teeth over my shoulder, biting down as I squeal. "Fuck, baby. If you don't let me have you, right now, I'm going to fucking explode."

"Take me, Ghost," I whisper, as he impatiently lifts me from the floor.

Without wasting another second, he lifts me up, locking my legs around his waist. He positions the tip of his cock at my entrance, and slowly sinks inside of me, inch by inch. Digging his fingertips into my lower back, bruising my skin, he moves within me.

His strokes become slow and torturous as his length consumes me. I'm already there, ready to come undone, as my breathing catches in my throat.

"I saved this just for you," I mumble against his mouth.

"Such a good girl," he sharply exhales, increasing the strength with each thrust.

My orgasm claims me, as my body begins to shake, and I cry out in ecstasy. My legs tremble as I grind my hips against him, working my clit at the same time, until my cries fade to soft, little whimpers.

Many thoughts rush through my mind, but there's only one that stands out. *I could get used to this.* But this is just for one night. One night only. By sunrise, it's over.

And that's what truly scares me.

Through the window, the sun's rays beam into the room. Ghost pulls me closer in his sleep, the muscles in his arm flexing as his grip on me tightens. Pressing my face in the crook of his neck, I breathe in the lingering, heady scent of his soap.

Suddenly, fear consumes me. It's morning. I'm too attached. I need to leave.

I need to leave now.

Carefully lifting his arm, I sneak away, trying my best not to wake him. Tiptoeing across the room, I catch a glimpse of myself in the mirror. What am I doing?

Shutting the door quietly behind me, I release a small breath, hating how I allowed myself to form such an unhealthy attachment to him. Walking down the quiet hallway, my heart hammers in my chest with each step, as I try not to wake anyone.

Until I realize I'm not alone.

Jason stands at the kitchen island, pouring himself a cup of coffee, and when he notices my presence, he becomes still. He knows. Placing the pot onto the granite counter, he frowns, seeming disheartened with my decision to leave.

"Before you sneak out, do you at least want some coffee?" he asks smugly.

Sheepishly dropping my gaze to the floor, I rub my face with my hands. "Shit," I mutter dryly. "I figured you would still be sleeping. I'm sorry."

"Coffee?" he reiterates, an edge to his tone.

"I'm okay—"

"Here." Jason walks around the island, gray sweatpants hung low on his hips. He hands me a canteen of hot coffee, locking his eyes with mine. "To go."

"I'm sorry," I anxiously blurt out, embarrassed.

"Is he awake?"

"No," I practically whisper. "He's still sleeping."

His face hardens. "He's not going to like this, Quinn," he presses, rubbing his fingers along his jaw. "He's going to lose his shit when he wakes up and you're not there."

"I told him that at sunrise, it's over."

He steps closer, catching me off guard. "But is that really what you want?" he asks.

My heart immediately sinks at the thought of losing him.

Losing all of them.

His eyes narrow. "Seems like you've already made up your mind," he points out. "Tell him. Tell him what you want. How you feel."

"It was just one night of fun," I try to convince myself. "I'm sure that he's going to wake up and forget all about me. That's how it usually works. I really have to go."

Bolting for the front door, I stop dead in my tracks, my hand lingering on the knob. Turning around one last time, our eyes lock in an intense stare.

"It was nice to meet you, Jason," I say.

"Likewise, Quinn," he replies, grinning crookedly.

I shut the door behind me.

The smell of a bonfire travels through the late afternoon air. My hair blows freely in the wind, as I anxiously tuck a loose strand behind my ear. My black combat boots crunch through the leaves covering the grass.

Walking up the front steps to the Salem public library, a smile claims my face. One of my favorite places to escape the world around me. Clutching my notebook tight against my chest, my gaze roams the library as I look for a quiet place to sit. My mind wanders, and I just can't seem to get everything that happened last night out of my head. No matter how hard I try, I can't stop thinking about them.

About Ghost.

I'd do anything to take back my *one night only* condition.

Sitting down at the table in the back of the building, I lean back in my chair. Opening my favorite romance novel, I breathe in the fresh, crisp pages. It's not fiction to me like it was before.

I can now say that I've lived out my darkest fantasies, and I have no regrets.

Flipping to the page where my bookmark rests, goosebumps rise on my skin, and the hair stands up on the back of my neck.

"You really thought I could let you go?"

He steps into my view, and my heart flutters. "Ghost."

He slips into the chair, sitting across from me at the table in what appears to be a wild state. Hair disheveled, eyes wide, dark bags beneath.

"I've been watching you from the distance for too long," he breathes.

A strong blush settles on my face, until it hits me. "You've been watching me?"

He nods. "Yes, I have."

"How?" I ask, my stomach immediately sinking. "For how long?"

"A while," he bleakly responds.

My eyebrows knit together, and I draw in a long breath once I finally connect the dots. He had looked so familiar last night when he had first taken off his mask because I've seen him before. Mainly, on campus, but also on several other occasions.

At the park. The mall. Downtown Salem, lurking in the distance.

I've seen him all over.

"And after having you last night, I'm keeping what I want. You're mine, *little Quinn*," he slowly lets out. "Say it."

Time seems to stop, and a sudden chill sweeps through me.

And without a doubt in my mind, I obey. "I'm yours."

ACKNOWLEDGEMENTS

Haley/daddy chaos

A simple "thank you" will never be enough. I mean it when I say I don't know how I ever did this without you. I appreciate you more than you will ever know. Every day you make a positive impact on my life and I'm so lucky to have you as not only my PA/editor/daddy/theres-too-much-to-name, but my very best friend

My incredible readers/friends

Thank you for giving me a life I look forward to waking up to each and every day. I wouldn't be able to live out my dreams without you all. Please know that your unconditional love and support means everything to me. Thank you for changing my life.

Paul

When I was just a little girl you once said "Molly, chase after your dreams. Do what makes you happy. You can be anything you want to be."

We did it, dad!!

Miss you

ABOUT THE AUTHOR

Molly Doyle has been writing since she was in grade school, and has been a published author since she was sixteen. Once she moved her talents to an online platform, her writing took off. She has reached millions of readers across the globe, with many of them crediting her for their mask kink. When she's not fantasizing about masked men, she's plotting her next erotic story.

ALSO BY MOLLY DOYLE

DESIRES DUET
DOMINANT DESIRES
DARK DESIRES

ORDER OF THE UNSEEN
SCREAM FOR US
BLOODSHED
MELT FOR US
BLOODBATH

SINNERS & SAINTS
SINNERS & SAINTS

Made in the USA
Coppell, TX
31 October 2023

23598124R00062